'I will go away, out of this dust and heat, out of this dry glitter of vanity, out of these toilsome futilities. I will go and never return.'

H. G. WELLS
Born 1866, Bromley, England
Died 1946, London, England

'A Slip under the Microscope' was first published in 1896 and
'The Door in the Wall' in 1906.

H. G. WELLS

A Slip under the Microscope

PENGUIN BOOKS

PENGUIN CLASSICS

Published by the Penguin Group
Penguin Books Ltd, 80 Strand, London WC2R ORL, England
Penguin Group (USA) Inc., 375 Hudson Street, New York, New York 10014, USA
Penguin Group (Canada), 90 Eglinton Avenue East, Suite 700, Toronto, Ontario,
Canada M4P 2Y3 (a division of Pearson Penguin Canada Inc.)
Penguin Ireland, 25 St Stephen's Green, Dublin 2, Ireland
(a division of Penguin Books Ltd)
Penguin Group (Australia), 707 Collins Street, Melbourne, Victoria 3008, Australia
(a division of Pearson Australia Group Pty Ltd)
Penguin Books India Pvt Ltd, 11 Community Centre, Panchsheel Park,
New Delhi – 110 017, India
Penguin Group (NZ), 67 Apollo Drive, Rosedale, Auckland 0632, New Zealand
(a division of Pearson New Zealand Ltd)
Penguin Books (South Africa) (Pty) Ltd, Block D, Rosebank Office Park,
181 Jan Smuts Avenue, Parktown North, Gauteng 2193, South Africa

Penguin Books Ltd, Registered Offices: 80 Strand, London WC2R ORL, England

www.penguin.com

This selection published in Penguin Classics 2015
001

Set in 9.5/13 pt Baskerville 10 Pro
Typeset by Jouve (UK), Milton Keynes
Printed in Great Britain by Clays Ltd, St Ives plc

A CIP catalogue record for this book is available from the British Library

ISBN: 978-0-141-39875-4

www.greenpenguin.co.uk

MIX
Paper from
responsible sources
FSC® C018179
www.fsc.org

Penguin Books is committed to a sustainable
future for our business, our readers and our planet.
This book is made from Forest Stewardship
Council™ certified paper.

Contents

The Door in the Wall

1

One confidential evening, not three months ago, Lionel
Wallace told me this story of the Door in the Wall. And
at the time I thought that so far as he was concerned it
was a true story.

He told it me with such a direct simplicity of conviction
that I could not do otherwise than believe in him. But in
the morning, in my own flat, I woke to a different atmosphere; and as I lay in bed and recalled the things he had
told me, stripped of the glamour of his earnest slow voice,
denuded of the focused, shaded table light, the shadowy
atmosphere that wrapped about him and me, and the
pleasant bright things, the dessert and glasses and napery
of the dinner we had shared, making them for the time
a bright little world quite cut off from everyday realities, I
saw it all as frankly incredible. 'He was mystifying!' I said,
and then: 'How well he did it! . . . It isn't quite the thing
I should have expected him, of all people, to do well.'

Afterwards as I sat up in bed and sipped my morning
tea, I found myself trying to account for the flavour of

reality that perplexed me in his impossible reminiscences, by supposing they did in some way suggest, present, convey – I hardly know which word to use – experiences it was otherwise impossible to tell.

Well, I don't resort to that explanation now. I have got over my intervening doubts. I believe now, as I believed at the moment of telling, that Wallace did to the very best of his ability strip the truth of his secret for me. But whether he himself saw, or only thought he saw, whether he himself was the possessor of an inestimable privilege or the victim of a fantastic dream, I cannot pretend to guess. Even the facts of his death, which ended my doubts for ever, throw no light on that.

That much the reader must judge for himself.

I forget now what chance comment or criticism of mine moved so reticent a man to confide in me. He was, I think, defending himself against an imputation of slackness and unreliability I had made in relation to a great public movement, in which he had disappointed me. But he plunged suddenly. 'I have,' he said, 'a preoccupation–

'I know,' he went on, after a pause, 'I have been negligent. The fact is – it isn't a case of ghosts or apparitions – but – it's an odd thing to tell of, Redmond – I am haunted. I am haunted by something – that rather takes the light out of things, that fills me with longings . . .'

He paused, checked by that English shyness that so often overcomes us when we would speak of moving or grave or beautiful things. 'You were at Saint Althelstan's all through,' he said, and for a moment that seemed to me quite irrelevant. 'Well' – and he paused. Then very haltingly at first, but afterwards more easily, he began to tell of the thing that was hidden in his life, the haunting memory of a beauty and a happiness that filled his heart with insatiable longings, that made all the interests and spectacle of worldly life seem dull and tedious and vain to him.

Now that I have the clue to it, the thing seems written visibly in his face. I have a photograph in which that look of detachment has been caught and intensified. It reminds me of what a woman once said of him – a woman who had loved him greatly. 'Suddenly,' she said, 'the interest goes out of him. He forgets you. He doesn't care a rap for you – under his very nose . . .'

Yet the interest was not always out of him, and when he was holding his attention to a thing Wallace could contrive to be an extremely successful man. His career, indeed, is set with successes. He left me behind him long ago; he soared up over my head, and cut a figure in the world that I couldn't cut – anyhow. He was still a year short of forty, and they say now that he would have been in office and very probably in the new Cabinet if he had lived. At school he always beat me without effort – as it were by nature. We were at school together at Saint Althelstan's College in West Kensington for almost all our school-time. He came into the school as my co-equal, but he left far above me, in a blaze of scholarships and brilliant performance. Yet I think I made a fair average running. And it was at school I heard first of the 'Door in the Wall' – that I was to hear of a second time only a month before his death.

To him at least the Door in the Wall was a real door, leading through a real wall to immortal realities. Of that I am now quite assured.

And it came into his life quite early, when he was a little fellow between five and six. I remember how, as he sat making his confession to me with a slow gravity, he reasoned and reckoned the date of it. 'There was,' he said, 'a crimson Virginia creeper in it – all one bright uniform crimson, in a clear amber sunshine against a white wall. That came into the impression somehow, though I don't clearly remember how, and there were horse-chestnut leaves upon the clean pavement outside the green door. They were blotched yellow and green, you know, not brown nor dirty, so that they must have been new fallen. I take it that means October. I look out for horse-chestnut leaves every year and I ought to know.

'If I'm right in that, I was about five years and four months old.'

He was, he said, rather a precocious little boy – he learnt to talk at an abnormally early age, and he was so sane and 'old-fashioned', as people say, that he was permitted an amount of initiative that most children scarcely attain by seven or eight. His mother died when he was two, and he was under the less vigilant and authoritative care of a nursery governess. His father was a stern, pre-occupied lawyer, who gave him little attention and expected great things of him. For all his brightness he found life grey and dull, I think. And one day he wandered.

He could not recall the particular neglect that enabled him to get away, nor the course he took among the West Kensington roads. All that had faded among the incurable blurs of memory. But the white wall and the green door stood out quite distinctly.

As his memory of that childish experience ran, he did at the very first sight of that door experience a peculiar emotion, an attraction, a desire to get to the door and open it and walk in. And at the same time he had the clearest conviction that either it was unwise or it was wrong of him – he could not tell which – to yield to this attraction. He insisted upon it as a curious thing that he knew from the very beginning – unless memory has played him the queerest trick – that the door was unfastened, and that he could go in as he chose.

I seem to see the figure of that little boy, drawn and repelled. And it was very clear in his mind, too, though why it should be so was never explained, that his father would be very angry if he went in through that door.

Wallace described all these moments of hesitation to

me with the utmost particularity. He went right past the door, and then, with his hands in his pockets and making an infantile attempt to whistle, strolled right along beyond the end of the wall. There he recalls a number of mean dirty shops, and particularly that of a plumber and decorator with a dusty disorder of earthenware pipes, sheet lead, ball taps, pattern books of wallpaper, and tins of enamel. He stood pretending to examine these things, and *coveting*, passionately desiring, the green door.

Then, he said, he had a gust of emotion. He made a run for it, lest hesitation should grip him again; he went plump with outstretched hand through the green door and let it slam behind him. And so, in a trice, he came into the garden that has haunted all his life.

It was very difficult for Wallace to give me his full sense of that garden into which he came.

There was something in the very air of it that exhilarated, that gave one a sense of lightness and good happening and well-being; there was something in the sight of it that made all its colour clean and perfect and subtly luminous. In the instant of coming into it one was exquisitely glad – as only in rare moments, and when one is young and joyful one can be glad in this world. And everything was beautiful there . . .

Wallace mused before he went on telling me. 'You see,' he said, with the doubtful inflection of a man who pauses at incredible things, 'there were two great panthers there . . . Yes, spotted panthers. And I was not afraid.

There was a long wide path with marble-edged flower borders on either side, and these two huge velvety beasts were playing there with a ball. One looked up and came towards me, a little curious as it seemed. It came right up to me, rubbed its soft round ear very gently against the small hand I held out, and purred. It was, I tell you, an enchanted garden. I know. And the size? Oh! it stretched far and wide, this way and that. I believe there were hills far away. Heaven knows where West Kensington had suddenly got to. And somehow it was just like coming home.

'You know, in the very moment the door swung to behind me, I forgot the road with its fallen chestnut leaves, its cabs and tradesmen's carts, I forgot the sort of gravitational pull back to the discipline and obedience of home, I forgot all hesitations and fear, forgot discretion, forgot all the intimate realities of this life. I became in a moment a very glad and wonder-happy little boy – in another world. It was a world with a different quality, a warmer, more penetrating and mellower light, with a faint clear gladness in its air, and wisps of sun-touched cloud in the blueness of its sky. And before me ran this long wide path, invitingly, with weedless beds on either side, rich with untended flowers, and these two great panthers. I put my little hands fearlessly on their soft fur, and caressed their round ears and the sensitive corners under their ears, and played with them, and it was as though they welcomed me home. There was a keen sense of home-coming in my mind, and when presently a tall, fair girl

7

appeared in the pathway and came to meet me, smiling, and said "Well?" to me, and lifted me and kissed me, and put me down and led me by the hand, there was no amazement, but only an impression of delightful rightness, of being reminded of happy things that had in some strange way been overlooked. There were broad red steps, I remember, that came into view between spikes of delphinium, and up these we went to a great avenue between very old and shady dark trees. All down this avenue, you know, between the red chapped stems, were marble seats of honour and statuary, and very tame and friendly white doves . . .

'Along this cool avenue my girl-friend led me, looking down – I recall the pleasant lines, the finely-modelled chin of her sweet kind face – asking me questions in a soft, agreeable voice, and telling me things, pleasant things I know, though what they were I was never able to recall . . . Presently a Capuchin monkey, very clean, with a fur of ruddy brown and kindly hazel eyes, came down a tree to us and ran beside me, looking up at me and grinning, and presently leapt to my shoulder. So we two went on our way in great happiness.'

He paused.

'Go on,' I said.

'I remember little things. We passed an old man musing among laurels, I remember, and a place gay with paroquets, and came through a broad shaded colonnade to a spacious cool palace, full of pleasant fountains, full of beautiful things, full of the quality and promise of heart's desire. And there were many things and many people, some that still seem to stand out clearly and some that are vaguer; but all these people were beautiful and kind. In some way – I don't know how – it was conveyed to me that they all were kind to me, glad to have me there, and filling me with gladness by their gestures, by the touch of their hands, by the welcome and love in their eyes. Yes—'

He mused for a while. 'Playmates I found there. That was very much to me, because I was a lonely little boy. They played delightful games in a grass-covered court where there was a sundial set about with flowers. And as one played one loved . . .

'But – it's odd – there's a gap in my memory. I don't remember the games we played. I never remembered. Afterwards, as a child, I spent long hours trying, even with tears, to recall the form of that happiness. I wanted to play it all over again – in my nursery – by myself. No! All I remember is the happiness and two dear playfellows who were most with me . . . Then presently came a sombre dark woman, with a grave, pale face and dreamy eyes, a sombre woman, wearing a soft long robe of pale purple, who carried a book, and beckoned and took me aside with her into a gallery above a hall – though my playmates were loth to have me go, and ceased their game and stood watching as I was carried away. "Come back to us!" they cried. "Come back to us soon!" I looked up

9

at her face, but she heeded them not at all. Her face was very gentle and grave. She took me to a seat in the gallery, and I stood beside her, ready to look at her book as she opened it upon her knee. The pages fell open. She pointed, and I looked, marvelling, for in the living pages of that book I saw myself; it was a story about myself, and in it were all the things that had happened to me since ever I was born . . .

'It was wonderful to me, because the pages of that book were not pictures, you understand, but realities.'

Wallace paused gravely – looked at me doubtfully.

'Go on,' I said. 'I understand.'

'They were realities – yes, they must have been; people moved and things came and went in them; my dear mother, whom I had near forgotten; then my father, stern and upright, the servants, the nursery, all the familiar things of home. Then the front door and the busy streets, with traffic to and fro. I looked and marvelled, and looked half doubtfully again into the woman's face and turned the pages over, skipping this and that, to see more of this book and more, and so at last I came to myself hovering and hesitating outside the green door in the long white wall, and felt again the conflict and the fear.

'"And next?" I cried, and would have turned on, but the cool hand of the grave woman delayed me.

'"Next?" I insisted, and struggled gently with her hand, pulling up her fingers with all my childish strength, and as she yielded and the page came over she bent down upon me like a shadow and kissed my brow.

'But the page did not show the enchanted garden, nor the panthers, nor the girl who had led me by the hand, nor the playfellows who had been so loth to let me go. It showed a long grey street in West Kensington, in that chill hour of afternoon before the lamps are lit; and I was there, a wretched little figure, weeping aloud, for all that I could do to restrain myself, and I was weeping because I could not return to my dear playfellows who had called after me, "Come back to us! Come back to us soon!" I was there. This was no page in a book, but harsh reality; that enchanted place and the restraining hand of the grave mother at whose knee I stood had gone – whither had they gone?'

He halted again, and remained for a time staring into the fire.

'Oh! the woefulness of that return!' he murmured.

'Well?' I said, after a minute or so.

'Poor little wretch I was! – brought back to this grey world again! As I realized the fullness of what had happened to me, I gave way to quite ungovernable grief. And the shame and humiliation of that public weeping and my disgraceful homecoming remain with me still. I see again the benevolent-looking old gentleman in gold spectacles who stopped and spoke to me – prodding me first with his umbrella. "Poor little chap," said he; "and are

you lost then?" – and me a London boy of five and more!
And he must needs bring in a kindly young policeman
and make a crowd of me, and so march me home. Sob-
bing, conspicuous, and frightened, I came back from the
enchanted garden to the steps of my father's house.

'That is as well as I can remember my vision of that
garden – the garden that haunts me still. Of course, I can
convey nothing of that indescribable quality of translu-
cent unreality, that *difference* from the common things of
experience that hung about it all; but that – that is what
happened. If it was a dream, I am sure it was a daytime
and altogether extraordinary dream . . . H'm! – naturally
there followed a terrible questioning, by my aunt, my
father, the nurse, the governess – everyone . . .

'I tried to tell them, and my father gave me my first
thrashing for telling lies. When afterwards I tried to tell
my aunt, she punished me again for my wicked persist-
ence. Then, as I said, everyone was forbidden to listen to
me, to hear a word about it. Even my fairy-tale books
were taken away from me for a time – because I was too
"imaginative". Eh? Yes, they did that! My father belonged
to the old school . . . And my story was driven back upon
myself. I whispered it to my pillow – my pillow that was
often damp and salt to my whispering lips with childish
tears. And I added always to my official and less fervent
prayers this one heartfelt request: "Please God I may
dream of the garden. Oh! take me back to my garden!"
Take me back to my garden! I dreamt often of the garden.

I may have added to it, I may have changed it; I do not know . . . All this, you understand, is an attempt to reconstruct from fragmentary memories a very early experience. Between that and the other consecutive memories of my boyhood there is a gulf. A time came when it seemed impossible I should ever speak of that wonder glimpse again.'

I asked an obvious question.

'No,' he said. 'I don't remember that I ever attempted to find my way back to the garden in those early years. This seems odd to me now, but I think that very probably a closer watch was kept on my movements after this misadventure to prevent my going astray. No, it wasn't till you knew me that I tried for the garden again. And I believe there was a period – incredible as it seems now – when I forgot the garden altogether – when I was about eight or nine it may have been. Do you remember me as a kid at Saint Althelstan's?'

'Rather!'

'I didn't show any signs, did I, in those days of having a secret dream?'

2

He looked up with a sudden smile.

'Did you ever play North-West Passage with me? . . . No, of course you didn't come my way!

'It was the sort of game,' he went on, 'that every imaginative child plays all day. The idea was the discovery of a North-West Passage to school. The way to school was plain enough; the game consisted in finding some way that wasn't plain, starting off ten minutes early in some almost hopeless direction, and working my way round through unaccustomed streets to my goal. And one day I got entangled among some rather low-class streets on the other side of Campden Hill, and I began to think that for once the game would be against me and that I should get to school late. I tried rather desperately a street that seemed a *cul-de-sac*, and found a passage at the end. I hurried through that with renewed hope. "I shall do it yet," I said, and passed a row of frowsy little shops that were inexplicably familiar to me, and behold! there was my long white wall and the green door that led to the enchanted garden!

'The thing whacked upon me suddenly. Then, after all, that garden, that wonderful garden, wasn't a dream!'

He paused.

'I suppose my second experience with the green door marks the world of difference there is between the busy life of a schoolboy and the infinite leisure of a child. Anyhow, this second time I didn't for a moment think of going in straight away. You see—. For one thing, my mind was full of the idea of getting to school in time – set on not breaking my record for punctuality. I must surely have felt *some* little desire at least to try the door – yes. I must have felt that . . . But I seem to remember the attraction of the door mainly as another obstacle to my overmastering determination to get to school. I was immensely interested by this discovery I had made, of course – I went on with my mind full of it – but I went on. It didn't check me. I ran past, tugging out my watch, found I had ten minutes still to spare, and then I was going downhill into familiar surroundings. I got to school, breathless, it is true, and wet with perspiration, but in time. I can remember hanging up my coat and hat . . . Went right by it and left it behind me. Odd, eh?'

He looked at me thoughtfully. 'Of course I didn't know then that it wouldn't always be there. Schoolboys have limited imaginations. I suppose I thought it was an awfully jolly thing to have it there, to know my way back to it; but there was the school tugging at me. I expect I was a good deal distraught and inattentive that morning, recalling what I could of the beautiful strange people I should presently see again. Oddly enough I had no doubt in my mind that they would be glad to see me . . . Yes, I must have thought of the garden that morning just as a jolly sort of place to which one might resort in the interludes of a strenuous scholastic career.

'I didn't go that day at all. The next day was a half-holiday, and that may have weighed with me. Perhaps, too, my state of inattention brought down impositions upon me, and

15

docked the margin of time necessary for the *détour*. I don't
know. What I do know is that in the meantime the
enchanted garden was so much upon my mind that I could
not keep it to myself.

'I told – what was his name? – a ferrety-looking youngster we used to call Squiff.'

'Young Hopkins,' said I.

'Hopkins it was. I did not like telling him. I had a feeling that in some way it was against the rules to tell him,
but I did. He was walking part of the way home with me;
he was talkative, and if we had not talked about the
enchanted garden we should have talked of something
else, and it was intolerable to me to think about any other
subject. So I blabbed.

'Well, he told my secret. The next day in the play inter-
val I found myself surrounded by half a dozen bigger
boys, half teasing, and wholly curious to hear more of
the enchanted garden. There was that big Fawcett – you
remember him? – and Carnaby and Morley Reynolds.
You weren't there by any chance? No, I think I should
have remembered if you were . . .

'A boy is a creature of odd feelings. I was, I really
believe, in spite of my secret self-disgust, a little flattered
to have the attention of these big fellows. I remember
particularly a moment of pleasure caused by the praise
of Crawshaw – you remember Crawshaw major, the son
of Crawshaw the composer? – who said it was the best

lie he had ever heard. But at the same time there was a really painful undertow of shame at telling what I felt was indeed a sacred secret. That beast Fawcett made a joke about the girl in green—'

Wallace's voice sank with the keen memory of that shame. 'I pretended not to hear,' he said. 'Well, then Carnaby suddenly called me a young liar, and disputed with me when I said the thing was true. I said I knew where to find the green door, could lead them all there in ten minutes. Carnaby became outrageously virtuous, and said I'd have to – and bear out my words or suffer. Did you ever have Carnaby twist your arm? Then perhaps you'll understand how it went with me. I swore my story was true. There was nobody in the school then to save a chap from Carnaby, though Crawshaw put in a word or so. Carnaby had got his game. I grew excited and red-eared, and a little frightened. I behaved altogether like a silly little chap, and the outcome of it all was that instead of starting alone for my enchanted garden, I led the way presently – cheeks flushed, ears hot, eyes smarting, and my soul one burning misery and shame – for a party of six mocking, curious, and threatening schoolfellows.

'We never found the white wall and the green door . . .'

'You mean—?'

'I mean I couldn't find it. I would have found it if I could.

'And afterwards when I could go alone I couldn't find

17

it. I never found it. I seem now to have been always looking for it through my schoolboy days, but I never came
upon it – never.'

'Did the fellows – make it disagreeable?'

'Beastly . . . Carnaby held a council over me for wanton
lying. I remember how I sneaked home and upstairs to
hide the marks of my blubbering. But when I cried myself
to sleep at last it wasn't for Carnaby, but for the garden,
for the beautiful afternoon I had hoped for, for the sweet
friendly women and the waiting playfellows, and the
game I had hoped to learn again, that beautiful forgotten
game . . .

'I believed firmly that if I had not told— . . . I had bad
times after that – crying at night and wool-gathering by
day. For two terms I slacked and had bad reports. Do you
remember? Of course you would! It was *you* – your beat-
ing me in mathematics that brought me back to the grind
again.'

3

For a time my friend stared silently into the red heart of
the fire. Then he said: 'I never saw it again until I was
seventeen.

'It leapt upon me for the third time – as I was driving
to Paddington on my way to Oxford and a scholarship.
I had just one momentary glimpse. I was leaning over the

apron of my hansom smoking a cigarette, and no doubt thinking myself no end of a man of the world, and suddenly there was the door, the wall, the dear sense of unforgettable and still attainable things.

'We clattered by – I too taken by surprise to stop my cab until we were well past and round a corner. Then I had a queer moment, a double and divergent movement of my will: I tapped the little door in the roof of the cab, and brought my arm down to pull out my watch. "Yes, sir!" said the cabman, smartly. "Er – well – it's nothing," I cried. "*My* mistake! We haven't much time! Go on!" And he went on . . .

'I got my scholarship. And the night after I was told of that I sat over my fire in my little upper room, my study, in my father's house, with his praise – his rare praise – and his sound counsels ringing in my ears, and I smoked my favourite pipe – the formidable bulldog of adolescence – and thought of that door in the long white wall. "If I had stopped," I thought, "I should have missed my scholarship, I should have missed Oxford – muddled all the fine career before me! I begin to see things better!" I fell musing deeply, but I did not doubt then this career of mine was a thing that merited sacrifice.

'Those dear friends and that clear atmosphere seemed very sweet to me, very fine but remote. My grip was fixing now upon the world. I saw another door opening – the door of my career.'

He stared again into the fire. Its red light picked out a

stubborn strength in his face for just one flickering moment, and then it vanished again.

'Well,' he said and sighed, 'I have served that career. I have done – much work, much hard work. But I have dreamt of the enchanted garden a thousand dreams, and seen its door, or at least glimpsed its door, four times since then. Yes – four times. For a while this world was so bright and interesting, seemed so full of meaning and opportunity, that the half-effaced charm of the garden was by comparison gentle and remote. Who wants to pat panthers on the way to dinner with pretty women and distinguished men? I came down to London from Oxford, a man of bold promise that I have done something to redeem. Something – and yet there have been disappointments . . .

'Twice I have been in love – I will not dwell on that – but once, as I went to someone who, I knew, doubted whether I dared to come, I took a short cut at a venture through an unfrequented road near Earl's Court, and so happened on a white wall and a familiar green door. "Odd!" said I to myself, "but I thought this place was on Campden Hill. It's the place I never could find somehow – like counting Stonehenge – the place of that queer daydream of mine." And I went by it intent upon my purpose. It had no appeal to me that afternoon.

'I had just a moment's impulse to try the door, three steps aside were needed at the most – though I was sure enough in my heart that it would open to me – and then

I thought that doing so might delay me on the way to that appointment in which my honour was involved. Afterwards I was sorry for my punctuality – I might at least have peeped in and waved a hand to those panthers, but I knew enough by this time not to seek again belatedly that which is not found by seeking. Yes, that time made me very sorry . . .

'Years of hard work after that, and never a sight of the door. It's only recently it has come back to me. With it there has come a sense as though some thin tarnish had spread itself over my world. I began to think of it as a sorrowful and bitter thing that I should never see that door again. Perhaps I was suffering a little from overwork – perhaps it was what I've heard spoken of as the feeling of forty. I don't know. But certainly the keen brightness that makes effort easy has gone out of things recently, and that just at a time – with all these new political developments – when I ought to be working. Odd, isn't it? But I do begin to find life toilsome, its rewards, as I come near them, cheap. I began a little while ago to want the garden quite badly. Yes – and I've seen it three times.'

'The garden?'

'No – the door! And I haven't gone in!'

He leant over the table to me, with an enormous sorrow in his voice as he spoke. 'Thrice I have had my chance – *thrice*! If ever that door offers itself to me again, I swore, I will go in, out of this dust and heat, out of this dry glitter of vanity, out of these toilsome futilities. I will go and never return. This time I will stay . . . I swore it, and when the time came – *I didn't go*.

'Three times in one year have I passed that door and failed to enter. Three times in the last year.

'The first time was on the night of the snatch division on the Tenants' Redemption Bill, on which the Government was saved by a majority of three. You remember? No one on our side – perhaps very few on the opposite side – expected the end that night. Then the debate collapsed like eggshells. I and Hotchkiss were dining with his cousin at Brentford; we were both unpaired, and we were called up by telephone, and set off at once in his cousin's motor. We got in barely in time, and on the way we passed my wall and door – livid in the moonlight, blotched with hot yellow as the glare of our lamps lit it, but unmistakable. "My God!" cried I. "What?" said Hotchkiss. "Nothing!" I answered, and the moment passed.

' "I've made a great sacrifice," I told the whip as I got in. "They all have," he said, and hurried by.

'I do not see how I could have done otherwise then. And the next occasion was as I rushed to my father's bedside to bid that stern old man farewell. Then, too, the claims of life were imperative. But the third time was different; it happened a week ago. It fills me with hot remorse to recall it. I was with Gurker and Ralphs – it's no secret now, you know, that I've had my talk with Gurker. We had been dining at Frobisher's, and the talk had become intimate between us. The question of my place in the reconstructed Ministry lay always just over the boundary of the discussion. Yes – yes. That's all settled. It needn't be talked about yet, but there's no reason to keep a secret from you . . . Yes – thanks! thanks! But let me tell you my story.

'Then, on that night things were very much in the air. My position was a very delicate one. I was keenly anxious to get some definite word from Gurker, but was hampered by Ralphs' presence. I was using the best power of my brain to keep that light and careless talk not too obviously directed to the point that concerned me. I had to. Ralphs' behaviour since has more than justified my caution . . . Ralphs, I knew, would leave us beyond the Kensington High Street, and then I could surprise Gurker by a sudden frankness. One has sometimes to resort to these little devices . . . And then it was that in the margin of my field of vision I became aware once more of the white wall, the green door before us down the road.

'We passed it talking. I passed it. I can still see the shadow of Gurker's marked profile, his opera hat tilted forward over his prominent nose, the many folds of his neck wrap going before my shadow and Ralphs' as we sauntered past.

'I passed within twenty inches of the door. "If I say goodnight to them, and go in," I asked myself, "what will happen?" And I was all a-tingle for that word with Gurker.

'I could not answer that question in the tangle of my other problems. "They will think me mad," I thought. "And suppose I vanish now! – Amazing disappearance of a prominent politician!" That weighed with me. A thousand inconceivably petty worldlinesses weighed with me in that crisis.'

Then he turned on me with a sorrowful smile, and, speaking slowly, 'Here I am!' he said.

'Here I am!' he repeated, 'and my chance has gone from me. Three times in one year the door has been offered me – the door that goes into peace, into delight, into a beauty beyond dreaming, a kindness no man on earth can know. And I have rejected it, Redmond, and it has gone—'

'How do you know?'

'I know. I know. I am left now to work it out, to stick to the tasks that held me so strongly when my moments came. You say I have success – this vulgar, tawdry, irksome, envied thing. I have it.' He had a walnut in his big hand. 'If that was my success,' he said, and crushed it, and held it out for me to see.

'Let me tell you something, Redmond. This loss is destroying me. For two months, for ten weeks nearly now, I have done no work at all, except the most necessary and urgent duties. My soul is full of inappeasable regrets. At nights – when it is less likely I shall be recognized – I go out. I wander. Yes. I wonder what people would think of that if they knew. A Cabinet Minister, the responsible head of that most vital of all departments, wandering alone – grieving – sometimes near audibly lamenting – for a door, for a garden!'

4

I can see now his rather pallid face, and the unfamiliar sombre fire that had come into his eyes. I see him very vividly tonight. I sit recalling his words, his tones, and last evening's *Westminster Gazette* still lies on my sofa, containing the notice of his death. At lunch today the club was busy with his death. We talked of nothing else.

They found his body very early yesterday morning in a deep excavation near East Kensington Station. It is one of two shafts that have been made in connection with an extension of the railway southward. It is protected from the intrusion of the public by a hoarding upon the high road, in which a small doorway has been cut for the convenience of some of the workmen who live in that direction. The doorway was left unfastened through a misunderstanding between two gangers, and through it he made his way.

My mind is darkened with questions and riddles.

It would seem he walked all the way from the House that night – he has frequently walked home during the past Session – and so it is I figure his dark form coming along the late and empty streets, wrapped up, intent. And then did the pale electric lights near the station cheat the rough planking into a semblance of white? Did that fatal unfastened door awaken some memory?

Was there, after all, ever any green door in the wall at all?

I do not know. I have told his story as he told it to me. There are times when I believe that Wallace was no more than the victim of the coincidence between a rare but not unprecedented type of hallucination and a careless trap, but that indeed is not my profoundest belief. You may think me superstitious, if you will, and foolish; but, indeed, I am more than half convinced that he had, in truth, an abnormal gift, and a sense, something – I know not what – that in the guise of wall and door offered him an outlet, a secret and peculiar passage of escape into another and altogether more beautiful world. At any rate, you will say, it betrayed him in the end. But did it betray him? There you touch the inmost mystery of these dreamers, these men of vision and the imagination. We see our world fair and common, the hoarding and the pit. By our daylight standard he walked out of security into darkness, danger, and death.

But did he see like that?

A Slip under the Microscope

Outside the laboratory windows was a watery-grey fog, and within a close warmth and the yellow light of the green-shaded gas lamps that stood two to each table down its narrow length. On each table stood a couple of glass jars containing the mangled vestiges of the crayfish, mussels, frogs, and guineapigs upon which the students had been working, and down the side of the room, facing the windows, were shelves bearing bleached dissections in spirits, surmounted by a row of beautifully executed anatomical drawings in whitewood frames and overhanging a row of cubical lockers. All the doors of the laboratory were panelled with blackboard, and on these were the half-erased diagrams of the previous day's work. The laboratory was empty, save for the demonstrator, who sat near the preparation-room door, and silent, save for a low, continuous murmur, and the clicking of the rocker microtome at which he was working. But scattered about the room were traces of numerous students: handbags, polished boxes of instruments, in one place a large drawing covered by newspaper, and in another a prettily bound copy of *News from Nowhere*, a book oddly at variance with its surroundings. These things had been put down hastily as the students had arrived and hurried at once to secure their seats in the adjacent lecture theatre. Deadened by the closed door, the measured accents of the professor sounded as a featureless muttering.

Presently, faint through the closed windows came the sound of the Oratory clock striking the hour of eleven. The clicking of the microtome ceased, and the demonstrator looked at his watch, rose, thrust his hands into his pockets, and walked slowly down the laboratory towards the lecture- theatre door. He stood listening for a moment, and then his eye fell on the little volume by William Morris. He picked it up, glanced at the title, smiled, opened it, looked at the name on the fly-leaf, ran the leaves through with his hand, and put it down. Almost immediately the even murmur of the lecturer ceased, there was a sudden burst of pencils rattling on the desks in the lecture theatre, a stirring, a scraping of feet, and a number of voices speaking together. Then a firm footfall approached the door, which began to open, and stood ajar as some indistinctly heard question arrested the newcomer.

The demonstrator turned, walked slowly back past the microtome, and left the laboratory by the preparation-room door. As he did so, first one, and then several students carrying notebooks entered the laboratory from the lecture theatre, and distributed themselves among the little tables, or stood in a group about the doorway. They were an exceptionally heterogeneous assembly, for while

Oxford and Cambridge still recoil from the blushing prospect of mixed classes, the College of Science anticipated America in the matter years ago – mixed socially too, for the prestige of the College is high, and its scholarships, free of any age limit, dredge deeper even than do those of the Scotch universities. The class numbered one-and-twenty, but some remained in the theatre questioning the professor, copying the blackboard diagrams before they were washed off, or examining the special specimens he had produced to illustrate the day's teaching. Of the nine who had come into the laboratory three were girls, one of whom, a little fair woman wearing spectacles and dressed in greyish-green, was peering out of the window at the fog, while the other two, both wholesome-looking, plain-faced schoolgirls, unrolled and put on the brown holland aprons they wore while dissecting. Of the men, two went down the laboratory to their places, one a pallid, dark-bearded man, who had once been a tailor; the other a pleasant-featured, ruddy young man of twenty, dressed in a well-fitting brown suit; young Wedderburn, the son of Wedderburn the eye specialist. The others formed a little knot near the theatre door. One of these, a dwarfed, spectacled figure with a hunchback, sat on a bent wood stool; two others, one a short, dark youngster and the other a flaxen-haired, reddish-complexioned young man, stood leaning side by side against the slate sink, while the fourth stood facing them, and maintained the larger share of the conversation.

This last person was named Hill. He was a sturdily built young fellow, of the same age as Wedderburn; he had a white face, dark grey eyes, hair of an indeterminate colour, and prominent, irregular features. He talked rather louder than was needful, and thrust his hands deeply into his pockets. His collar was frayed and blue with the starch of a careless laundress, his clothes were evidently ready-made, and there was a patch on the side of his boot near the toe. And as he talked or listened to the others, he glanced now and again towards the lecture-theatre door. They were discussing the depressing peroration of the lecture they had just heard, the last lecture it was in the introductory course in zoology. 'From ovum to ovum is the goal of the higher vertebrata,' the lecturer had said in his melancholy tones, and so had neatly rounded off the sketch of comparative anatomy he had been developing. The spectacled hunchback had repeated it with noisy appreciation, had tossed it towards the fair-haired student with an evident provocation, and had started one of those vague, rambling discussions on generalities so unaccountably dear to the student mind all the world over.

'That is our goal, perhaps – I admit it, as far as science goes,' said the fair-haired student, rising to the challenge. 'But there are things above science.'

'Science,' said Hill confidently, 'is systematic knowledge. Ideas that don't come into the system – must anyhow – be loose ideas.' He was not quite sure whether that was a clever saying or a fatuity until his hearers took it seriously.

'The thing I cannot understand,' said the hunchback, at large, 'is whether Hill is a materialist or not.'

'There is one thing above matter,' said Hill promptly, feeling he made a better point this time, aware, too, of someone in the doorway behind him, and raising his voice a trifle for her benefit, 'and that is, the delusion that there is something above matter.'

'So we have your gospel at last,' said the fair student. 'It's all a delusion, is it? All our aspirations to lead something more than dogs' lives, all our work for anything beyond ourselves. But see how inconsistent you are. Your socialism, for instance. Why do you trouble about the interests of the race? Why do you concern yourself about the beggar in the gutter? Why are you bothering yourself to lend that book' – he indicated William Morris by a movement of the head – 'to everyone in the lab?'

'Girl,' said the hunchback indistinctly, and glanced guiltily over his shoulder.

The girl in brown, with the brown eyes, had come into the laboratory, and stood on the other side of the table behind him, with her rolled-up apron in one hand, looking over her shoulder, listening to the discussion. She did not notice the hunchback, because she was glancing from Hill to his interlocutor. Hill's consciousness of her presence betrayed itself to her only in his studious ignoring of the fact; but she understood that, and it pleased her. 'I see no reason,' said he, 'why a man should live like a brute because he knows of nothing beyond matter, and does not expect to exist a hundred years hence.'

'Why shouldn't he?' said the fair-haired student.

'Why *should* he?' said Hill.

'What inducement has he?'

'That's the way with all you religious people. It's all a business of inducements. Cannot a man seek after righteousness for righteousness' sake?'

There was a pause. The fair man answered, with a kind of vocal padding, 'But – you see – inducement – when I said inducement,' to gain time. And then the hunchback came to his rescue and inserted a question. He was a terrible person in the debating society with his questions, and they invariably took one form – a demand for a definition. 'What's your definition of righteousness?' said the hunchback at this stage.

Hill experienced a sudden loss of complacency at this question, but even as it was asked, relief came in the person of Brooks, the laboratory attendant, who entered by the preparation-room door, carrying a number of freshly killed guineapigs by their hind legs. 'This is the last batch of material this session,' said the youngster who had not previously spoken. Brooks advanced up the laboratory, smacking down a couple of guineapigs at each table. The rest of the class, scenting the prey from afar, came crowding in by the lecture theatre door, and the discussion perished abruptly as the students who were not already in their places hurried to them to secure the choice of a specimen. There was a noise of keys rattling on split rings as lockers were opened and dissecting instruments taken out. Hill was already standing by his table, and his box of scalpels was sticking out of his pocket. The girl in brown came a step towards him, and leaning over his table said softly, 'Did you see that I returned your book, Mr Hill?'

During the whole scene she and the book had been vividly present in his consciousness; but he made a clumsy pretence of looking at the book and seeing it for the first time. 'Oh yes,' he said, taking it up. 'I see. Did you like it?'

'I want to ask you some questions about it – sometime.'

'Certainly,' said Hill. 'I shall be glad.' He stopped awkwardly. 'You liked it?' he said.

'It's a wonderful book. Only some things I don't understand.'

Then suddenly the laboratory was hushed by a curious braying noise. It was the demonstrator. He was at the blackboard ready to begin the day's instruction, and it was his custom to demand silence by a sound midway between the 'Er' of common intercourse and the blast of a trumpet. The girl in brown slipped back to her place: it was immediately in front of Hill's, and Hill, forgetting her forthwith, took a notebook out of the drawer of his table, turned over its leaves hastily, drew a stumpy pencil from his pocket, and prepared to make a copious note of the coming demonstration. For demonstrations and lectures are the sacred text of the College students. Books, saving only the Professor's own, you may – it is even expedient to – ignore.

Hill was the son of a Landport cobbler, and had been hooked by a chance blue paper the authorities had thrown out to the Landport Technical College. He kept himself in London on his allowance of a guinea a week, and found that, with proper care, this also covered his clothing allowance, an occasional waterproof collar, that is; and ink and needles and cotton and such-like necessaries for a man about town. This was his first year and his first session, but the brown old man in Landport had already got himself detested in many public-houses by boasting of his son, 'the Professor'. Hill was a vigorous youngster, with a serene contempt for the clergy of all denominations, and a fine ambition to reconstruct the world. He regarded his scholarship as a brilliant opportunity. He had begun to read at seven, and had read steadily whatever came in his way, good or bad, since then. His worldly experience had been limited to the island of Portsea, and acquired chiefly in the wholesale boot factory in which he had worked by day, after passing the seventh standard of the Board school. He had a considerable gift of speech, as the College Debating Society, which met amidst the crushing machines and mine models in the metallurgical theatre downstairs, already recognized – recognized by a violent battering of desks whenever he rose. And he was just at that fine emotional age when life opens at the end of a narrow pass like a broad valley at one's feet, full of the promise of wonderful discoveries and tremendous achievements. And his own limitations, save that he knew that he knew neither Latin nor French, were all unknown to him.

At first his interest had been divided pretty equally between his biological work at the College and social and theological theorizing, an employment which he took in deadly earnest. Of a night, when the big museum library was not open, he would sit on the bed of his room in Chelsea with his coat and a muffler on, and write out the lecture notes and revise his dissection memoranda until Thorpe called him out by a whistle – the landlady objected to open the door to attic visitors – and then the two would go prowling about the shadowy, shiny, gaslit streets, talking, very much in the fashion of the sample just given, of the God Idea and Righteousness and Carlyle and the Reorganization of Society. And in the midst of it all, Hill, arguing not only for Thorpe but for the casual passer-by, would lose the thread of his argument glancing at some pretty painted face that looked meaningly at him as he passed. Science and Righteousness! But once or twice lately there had been signs that a third interest was creeping into his life, and he had found his attention wandering from the fate of the mesoblastic somites or the probable meaning of the blastopore, to the thought of the girl with the brown eyes who sat at the table before him.

She was a paying student; she descended inconceivable social altitudes to speak to him. At the thought of the education she must have had, and the accomplishments she must possess, the soul of Hill became abject within him. She had spoken to him first over a difficulty about the alisphenoid of a rabbit's skull, and he had found that, in biology at least, he had no reason for self-abasement. And from that, after the manner of young people starting from any starting-point, they got to generalities, and while Hill attacked her upon the question of socialism, – some instinct told him to spare her a direct assault upon her religion – she was gathering resolution to undertake what she told herself was his aesthetic education. She was a year or two older than he, though the thought never occurred to him. The loan of *News from Nowhere* was the beginning of a series of cross loans. Upon some absurd first principle of his, Hill had never 'wasted time' upon poetry, and it seemed an appalling deficiency to her. One day in the lunch hour, when she chanced upon him alone in the little museum where the skeletons were arranged, shamefully eating the bun that constituted his midday meal, she retreated, and returned to lend him, with a slightly furtive air, a volume of Browning. He stood sideways towards her and took the book rather clumsily, because he was holding the bun in the other hand. And in the retrospect his voice lacked the cheerful clearness he could have wished.

That occurred after the examination in comparative anatomy, on the day before the College turned out its students and was carefully locked up by the officials for the Christmas holidays. The excitement of cramming for the first trial of strength had for a little while dominated Hill to the exclusion of his other interests. In the forecasts of the result in which everyone indulged he was surprised to find that no one regarded him as a possible competitor for the Harvey Commemoration Medal, of which this and the two subsequent examinations disposed. It was about this time that Wedderburn, who so far had lived inconspicuously on the uttermost margin of Hill's perceptions, began to take on the appearance of an obstacle. By a mutual agreement, the nocturnal prowlings with Thorpe ceased for the three weeks before the examination, and his landlady pointed out that she really could not supply so much lamp oil at the price. He walked to and fro from the College with little slips of mnemonics in his hand, lists of crayfish appendages, rabbits' skull-bones, and vertebrate nerves, for example, and became a positive nuisance to foot passengers in the opposite direction.

But, by a natural reaction, Poetry and the girl with the brown eyes ruled the Christmas holiday. The pending results of the examination became such a secondary consideration that Hill marvelled at his father's excitement.

Even had he wished it, there was no comparative anatomy to read in Landport, and he was too poor to buy books, but the stock of poets in the library was extensive, and Hill's attack was magnificently sustained. He saturated himself with the fluent numbers of Longfellow and Tennyson, and fortified himself with Shakespeare; found a kindred soul in Pope and a master in Shelley, and heard and fled the siren voices of Eliza Cook and Mrs Hemans. But he read no more Browning, because he hoped for the loan of other volumes from Miss Haysman when he returned to London.

He walked from his lodgings to the College with that volume of Browning in his shiny black bag, and his mind teeming with the finest general propositions about poetry. Indeed, he framed first this little speech and then that with which to grace the return. The morning was an exceptionally pleasant one for London; there was a clear hard frost and undeniable blue in the sky, a thin haze softened every outline, and warm shafts of sunlight struck between the house blocks and turned the sunny side of the street to amber and gold. In the hall of the College he pulled off his glove and signed his name with fingers so stiff with cold that the characteristic dash under the signature he cultivated became a quivering line. He imagined Miss Haysman about him everywhere. He turned at the staircase, and there, below, he saw a crowd struggling at the foot of the noticeboard. This, possibly, was the biology list. He forgot Browning and Miss Haysman for the moment, and joined the scrimmage. And at last, with his cheek flattened against the sleeve of the man on the step above him, he read the list –

CLASS I
H. J. Somers Wedderburn
William Hill

and thereafter followed a second class that is outside our present sympathies. It was characteristic that he did not trouble to look for Thorpe on the physics list, but backed out of the struggle at once, and in a curious emotional state between pride over common second-class humanity and acute disappointment at Wedderburn's success, went on his way upstairs. At the top, as he was hanging up his coat in the passage, the zoological demonstrator, a young man from Oxford who secretly regarded him as a blatant 'mugger' of the very worst type, offered his heartiest congratulations.

At the laboratory door Hill stopped for a second to get his breath, and then entered. He looked straight up the laboratory and saw all five girl students grouped in their places, and Wedderburn, the once retiring Wedderburn, leaning rather gracefully against the window, playing with the blind tassel and talking apparently to the five of them. Now, Hill could talk bravely enough and even overbearingly to one girl, and he could have made a speech to a roomful of girls, but this business of standing at ease and appreciating, fencing, and returning quick remarks round a group was, he knew, altogether beyond him. Coming up the staircase his feelings for Wedderburn had been generous, a certain admiration perhaps, a willingness to shake his hand conspicuously and heartily as one who had fought but the first round. But before Christmas Wedderburn had never gone up to that end of the room to talk. In a flash Hill's mist of vague excitement condensed abruptly to a vivid dislike of Wedderburn. Possibly his expression changed. As he came up to his place, Wedderburn nodded carelessly to him, and the others glanced round. Miss Haysman looked at him and away again, the faintest touch of her eyes. 'I can't agree with you, Mr Wedderburn,' she said.

'I must congratulate you on your first class, Mr Hill,' said the spectacled girl in green, turning round and beaming at him.

'It's nothing,' said Hill, staring at Wedderburn and Miss Haysman talking together, and eager to hear what they talked about.

'We poor folks in the second class don't think so,' said the girl in spectacles.

What was it Wedderburn was saying? Something about William Morris! Hill did not answer the girl in spectacles, and the smile died out of his face. He could not hear, and failed to see how he could 'cut in'. Confound Wedderburn! He sat down, opened his bag, hesitated whether to return the volume of Browning forthwith, in the sight of all, and instead drew out his new notebooks for the short course in elementary botany that was now beginning, and which would terminate in February. As he did so, a fat heavy man with a white face and pale grey eyes – Bindon, the professor of botany, who came up from Kew for January and February – came in by the lecture-theatre door, and passed, rubbing his hands together and smiling, in silent affability down the laboratory.

In the subsequent six weeks Hill experienced some very rapid and curiously complex emotional developments. For the most part he had Wedderburn in focus – a fact that Miss Haysman never suspected. She told Hill (for in the comparative privacy of the museum she talked a good deal to him of socialism and Browning and general propositions) that she had met Wedderburn at the house of some people she knew, and 'he's inherited his cleverness; for his father, you know, is the great eye specialist'.

'*My* father is a cobbler,' said Hill, quite irrelevantly, and perceived the want of dignity even as he said it. But the gleam of jealousy did not offend her. She conceived herself the fundamental source of it. He suffered bitterly from a sense of Wedderburn's unfairness, and a realization of his own handicap. Here was this Wedderburn had picked up a prominent man for a father, and instead of his losing so many marks on the score of that advantage, it was counted to him for righteousness! And while Hill had to introduce himself and talk to Miss Haysman

41

clumsily over mangled guineapigs in the laboratory, this Wedderburn, in some backstairs way, had access to her social altitudes, and could converse in a polished argot that Hill understood perhaps, but felt incapable of speaking. Not, of course, that he wanted to. Then it seemed to Hill that for Wedderburn to come there day after day with cuffs unfrayed, neatly tailored, precisely barbered, quietly perfect, was in itself an ill-bred, sneering sort of proceeding. Moreover, it was a stealthy thing for Wedderburn to behave insignificantly for a space, to mock modesty, to lead Hill to fancy that he himself was beyond dispute the man of the year, and then suddenly to dart in front of him, and incontinently to swell up in this fashion. In addition to these things, Wedderburn displayed an increasing disposition to join in any conversational grouping that included Miss Haysman; and would venture, and indeed seek occasion, to pass opinions derogatory to socialism and atheism. He goaded Hill to incivilities by neat, shallow, and exceedingly effective personalities about the socialist leaders, until Hill hated Bernard Shaw's graceful egotisms, William Morris's limited editions and luxurious wallpapers, and Walter Crane's charmingly absurd ideal working men, about as much as he hated Wedderburn. The dissertations in the laboratory, that had been his glory in the previous term, became a danger, degenerated into inglorious tussles with Wedderburn, and Hill kept to them only out of an obscure perception that his honour was involved. In the debating

society Hill knew quite clearly that, to a thunderous
accompaniment of banged desks, he could have pulverized Wedderburn. Only Wedderburn never attended the
debating society to be pulverized, because – nauseous
affectation! – he 'dined late'.

You must not imagine that these things presented themselves in quite such a crude form to Hill's perception. Hill
was a born generalizer. Wedderburn to him was not so
much an individual obstacle as a type, the salient angle
of a class. The economic theories that, after infinite ferment,
had shaped themselves in Hill's mind, became abruptly
concrete at the contact. The world became full of
easy-mannered, graceful, gracefully dressed, conversation-
ally dexterous, finally shallow Wedderburns, Bishops
Wedderburn, Wedderburn M.P.s, Professors Wedderburn, Wedderburn landlords, all with finger-bowl
shibboleths and epigrammatic cities of refuge from a
sturdy debater. And everyone ill-clothed or ill-dressed,
from the cobbler to the cab-runner, was, to Hill's imagination, a man and a brother, a fellow-sufferer. So that he
became, as it were, a champion of the fallen and oppressed,
albeit to outward seeming only a self-assertive, ill-
mannered young man, and an unsuccessful champion at
that. Again and again a skirmish over the afternoon tea
that the girl students had inaugurated left Hill with
flushed cheeks and a tattered temper, and the debating
society noticed a new quality of sarcastic bitterness in his
speeches.

You will understand now how it was necessary, if only in the interests of humanity, that Hill should demolish Wedderburn in the forthcoming examination and out-shine him in the eyes of Miss Haysman; and you will perceive, too, how Miss Haysman fell into some common feminine misconceptions. The Hill–Wedderburn quarrel, for in his unostentatious way Wedderburn reciprocated Hill's ill-veiled rivalry, became a tribute to her indefinable charm: she was the Queen of Beauty in a tournament of scalpels and stumpy pencils. To her confidential friend's secret annoyance, it even troubled her conscience, for she was a good girl, and painfully aware, through Ruskin and contemporary fiction, how entirely men's activities are determined by women's attitudes. And if Hill never by any chance mentioned the topic of love to her, she only credited him with the finer modesty for that omission.

So the time came on for the second examination, and Hill's increasing pallor confirmed the general rumour that he was working hard. In the aerated bread shop near South Kensington Station you would see him, breaking his bun and sipping his milk with his eyes intent upon a paper of closely written notes. In his bedroom there were propositions about buds and stems round his looking-glass, a diagram to catch his eye, if soap should chance to spare it, above his washing basin. He missed several meetings of the debating society, but he found the chance encounters with Miss Haysman in the spacious ways of the adjacent art museum, or in the little museum at the top of the College, or in the College corridors, more frequent and very restful. In particular, they used to meet in a little gallery full of wrought-iron chests and gates near the art library, and there Hill used to talk, under the gentle stimulus of her flattering attention, of Browning and his personal ambitions. A characteristic she found remarkable in him was his freedom from avarice. He contemplated quite calmly the prospect of living all his life on an income below a hundred pounds a year. But he was determined to be famous, to make, recognizably in his own proper person, the world a better place to live in. He took Bradlaugh and John Burns for his leaders and models, poor, even impecunious, great men. But Miss Haysman thought that such lives were deficient on the aesthetic side, by which, though she did not know it, she meant good wallpaper and upholstery, pretty books, tasteful clothes, concerts, and meals nicely cooked and respectfully served.

At last came the day of the second examination, and the professor of botany, a fussy, conscientious man, rearranged all the tables in a long narrow laboratory to prevent copying, and put his demonstrator on a chair on a table (where he felt, he said, like a Hindu god), to see all the cheating, and stuck a notice outside the door, 'Door closed', for no earthly reason that any human being could discover. And all the morning from ten till one the quill of Wedderburn shrieked defiance at Hill's, and the quills of the others chased their leaders in a tireless pack, and so also it was in the afternoon. Wedderburn was a little quieter than usual, and Hill's face was hot all day, and his overcoat bulged with textbooks and notebooks against the last moment's revision. And the next day, in the morning and in the afternoon, was the practical examination, when sections had to be cut and slides identified. In the morning Hill was depressed because he knew he had cut a thick section, and in the afternoon came the mysterious slip.

It was just the kind of thing that the botanical professor was always doing. Like the income tax, it offered a premium to the cheat. It was a preparation under the microscope, a little glass slip, held in its place on the stage of the instrument by light steel clips, and the inscription set forth that the slip was not to be moved. Each student was to go in turn to it, sketch it, write in his book of answers what he considered it to be, and return to his place. Now, to move such a slip is a thing one can do by a chance movement of the finger, and in a fraction of a second. The professor's reason for decreeing that the slip should not be moved depended on the fact that the object he wanted identified was characteristic of a certain tree-stem. In the position in which it was placed it was a difficult thing to recognize, but once the slip was moved so as to bring other parts of the preparation into view, its nature was obvious enough.

Hill came to this, flushed from a contest with staining reagents, sat down on the little stool before the microscope, turned the mirror to get the best light, and then, out of sheer habit, shifted the slip. At once he remembered the prohibition, and, with an almost continuous motion of his hands, moved it back, and sat paralysed with astonishment at his action.

Then, slowly, he turned his head. The professor was out of the room; the demonstrator sat aloft on his impromptu rostrum, reading the *Q. Jour. Mi. Sci.*; the rest of the examinees were busy, and with their backs to him. Should he own up to the accident now? He knew quite clearly what the thing was. It was a lenticel, a characteristic preparation from the elder-tree. His eyes roved over his intent fellow-students and Wedderburn suddenly glanced over his shoulder at him with a queer expression in his eyes. The mental excitement that had kept Hill at an abnormal pitch of vigour these two days gave way to a curious nervous tension. His book of answers was beside him. He did not write down what the thing was, but with one eye at the microscope he began making a hasty sketch of it. His mind was full of this grotesque puzzle in ethics that had suddenly been sprung upon him. Should he identify it? or should he leave this question unanswered? In that case Wedderburn would probably come out first in the second result. How could he tell now whether he might not have identified the thing without shifting it? It was possible that Wedderburn had failed to recognize it, of course. Suppose Wedderburn too had shifted the slide? He looked up at the clock. There were fifteen minutes in which to make up his mind. He gathered up his book of answers and the coloured pencils he used in illustrating his replies and walked back to his seat.

He read through his manuscript, and then sat thinking and gnawing his knuckle. It would look queer now if he owned up. He *must* beat Wedderburn. He forgot the examples of those starry gentlemen, John Burns and Bradlaugh. Besides, he reflected, the glimpse of the rest of the slip he had had was after all quite accidental, forced upon him by chance, a kind of providential revelation rather than an unfair advantage. It was not nearly so dishonest to avail himself of that as it was of Broome, who believed in the efficacy of prayer, to pray daily for a first-class. 'Five minutes more,' said the demonstrator, folding up his paper and becoming observant. Hill watched the clock hands until two minutes remained; then he opened the book of answers, and, with hot ears and an affectation of ease, gave his drawing of the lenticel its name.

When the second pass list appeared, the previous positions of Wedderburn and Hill were reversed, and the spectacled girl in green, who knew the demonstrator in private life (where he was practically human), said that in the result of the two examinations taken together Hill had the advantage of a mark – 167 to 166 out of a possible 200. Everyone admired Hill in a way, though the suspicion of 'mugging' clung to him. But Hill was to find congratulations and Miss Haysman's enhanced opinion of him, and even the decided decline in the crest of

Wedderburn, tainted by an unhappy memory. He felt a remarkable access of energy at first, and the note of a democracy marching to triumph returned to his debating society speeches; he worked at his comparative anatomy with tremendous zeal and effect, and he went on with his aesthetic education. But through it all, a vivid little picture was continually coming before his mind's eye – of a sneakish person manipulating a slide.

No human being had witnessed the act, and he was cocksure that no higher power existed to see it; but for all that it worried him. Memories are not dead things, but alive; they dwindle in disuse, but they harden and develop in all sorts of queer ways if they are being continually fretted. Curiously enough, though at the time he perceived clearly that the shifting was accidental, as the days wore on his memory became confused about it, until at last he was not sure – although he assured himself that he *was* sure – whether the movement had been absolutely involuntary. Then it is possible that Hill's dietary was conducive to morbid conscientiousness; a breakfast frequently eaten in a hurry, a midday bun, and, at such hours after five as chanced to be convenient, such meat as his means determined, usually in a chop-house in a back street off the Brompton Road. Occasionally he treated himself to threepenny or ninepenny classics, and they usually represented a suppression of potatoes or chops. It is indisputable that outbreaks of self-abasement and emotional revival have a distinct relation to periods of scarcity. But apart from this influence on the feelings, there was in Hill a distinct aversion to falsity that the blasphemous Landport cobbler had inculcated by strap and tongue from his earliest years. Of one fact about professed atheists I am convinced; they may be – they usually are – fools, void of subtlety, revilers of holy institutions, brutal speakers, and mischievous knaves, but they lie with difficulty. If it were not so, if they had the faintest grasp of the idea of compromise, they would simply be liberal churchmen. And, moreover, this memory poisoned his regard for Miss Haysman. For she now so evidently preferred him to Wedderburn that he felt sure he cared for her, and began reciprocating her attentions by timid marks of personal regard; at one time he even bought a bunch of violets, carried it about in his pocket, and produced it with a stumbling explanation, withered and dead, in the gallery of old iron. It poisoned, too, the denunciation of capitalist dishonesty that had been one of his life's pleasures. And, lastly, it poisoned his triumph in Wedderburn. Previously he had been Wedderburn's superior in his own eyes, and had raged simply at a want of recognition. Now he began to fret at the darker suspicion of positive inferiority. He fancied he found justifications for his position in Browning, but they vanished on analysis. At last – moved, curiously enough, by exactly the same motive forces that had resulted in his dishonesty – he went to Professor Bindon, and made a clean breast of the whole affair. As Hill was a paid student, Professor Bindon did not ask him to sit down, and he stood before the professor's desk as he made his confession.

'It's a curious story,' said Professor Bindon, slowly realizing how the thing reflected on himself, and then letting his anger rise, – 'A most remarkable story. I can't understand your doing it, and I can't understand this avowal. You're a type of student – Cambridge men would never dream – I suppose I ought to have thought – Why *did* you cheat?'

'I didn't cheat,' said Hill.

'But you have just been telling me you did.'

'I thought I explained–'

'Either you cheated or you did not cheat.'–

'I said my motion was involuntary.'

'I am not a metaphysician, I am a servant of science – of fact. You were told not to move the slip. You did move the slip. If that is not cheating–'

'If I was a cheat,' said Hill, with the note of hysterics in his voice, 'should I come here and tell you?'

'Your repentance, of course, does you credit,' said Professor Bindon, 'but it does not alter the original facts.'

'No, sir,' said Hill, giving in in utter self-abasement.

'Even now you cause an enormous amount of trouble. The examination list will have to be revised.'

'I suppose so, sir.'

'Suppose so? Of course it must be revised. And I don't see how I can conscientiously pass you.'

'Not pass me?' said Hill. 'Fail me?'

'It's the rule in all examinations. Or where should we be? What else did you expect? You don't want to shirk the consequences of your own acts?'

'I thought, perhaps' – said Hill. And then, 'Fail me? I thought, as I told you, you would simply deduct the marks given for that slip.'

'Impossible!' said Bindon. 'Besides, it would still leave you above Wedderburn. Deduct only the marks – Preposterous! The Departmental Regulations distinctly say–'

'But it's my own admission, sir.'

'The Regulations say nothing whatever of the manner in which the matter comes to light. They simply provide–'

'It will ruin me. If I fail this examination, they won't renew my scholarship.'

'You should have thought of that before.'

'But, sir, consider all my circumstances–'

'I cannot consider anything. Professors in this College are machines. The Regulations will not even let us recommend our students for appointments. I am a machine, and you have worked me. I have to do–'

'It's very hard, sir.'

'Possibly it is.'

'If I am to be failed this examination, I might as well go home at once.'

'That is as you think proper.' Bindon's voice softened a little; he perceived he had been unjust, and, provided he did not contradict himself, he was disposed to amelioration. 'As a private person,' he said, 'I think this confession of yours goes far to mitigate your offence. But you have set the machinery in motion, and now it must take its course. I – I am really sorry you gave way.'

A wave of emotion prevented Hill from answering. Suddenly, very vividly, he saw the heavily lined face of the old Landport cobbler, his father. 'Good God! What a fool I have been!' he said hotly and abruptly.

'I hope,' said Bindon, 'that it will be a lesson to you.'

But, curiously enough, they were not thinking of quite the same indiscretion.

There was a pause.

'I would like a day to think, sir, and then I will let you know – about going home, I mean,' said Hill, moving towards the door.

The next day Hill's place was vacant. The spectacled girl in green was, as usual, first with the news. Wedderburn and Miss Haysman were talking of a performance of *The Meistersingers* when she came up to them.

'Have you heard?' she said.

'Heard what?'

'There was cheating in the examination.'

'Cheating!' said Wedderburn, with his face suddenly hot. 'How?'

'That slide'–

'Moved? Never!'

'It was. That slide that we weren't to move'–

'Nonsense!' said Wedderburn. 'Why! How could they find out? Who do they say–?'

'It was Mr Hill.'

'*Hill!*'

'Mr Hill!'

'Not – surely not the immaculate Hill?' said Wedderburn, recovering.

'I don't believe it,' said Miss Haysman. 'How do you know?'

'I *didn't*,' said the girl in spectacles. 'But I know it now for a fact. Mr Hill went and confessed to Professor Bindon himself.'

'By Jove!' said Wedderburn. 'Hill of all people. But I am always inclined to distrust these philanthropists-on-principle' –

'Are you quite sure?' said Miss Haysman, with a catch in her breath.

'Quite. It's dreadful, isn't it? But, you know, what can you expect? His father is a cobbler.'

Then Miss Haysman astonished the girl in spectacles.

'I don't care. I will not believe it,' she said, flushing darkly under her warm-tinted skin. 'I will not believe it until he has told me so himself – face to face. I would scarcely believe it then,' and abruptly she turned her back on the girl in spectacles, and walked to her own place.

'It's true, all the same,' said the girl in spectacles, peering and smiling at Wedderburn.

But Wedderburn did not answer her. She was indeed one of those people who seem destined to make unanswered remarks.